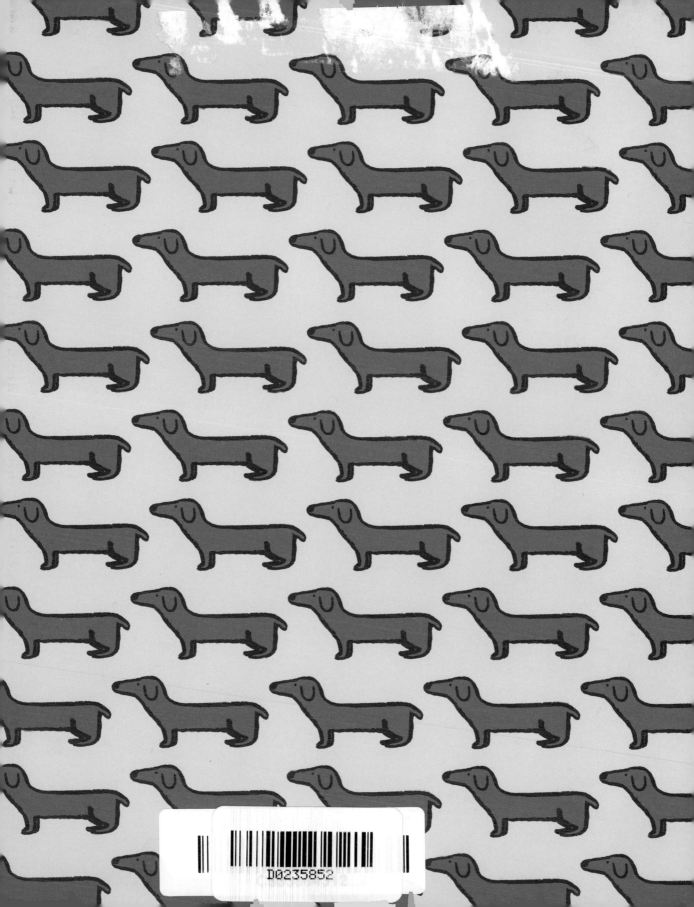

To Sarah
J.J.

Ralf

First edition 2014
Text and illustrations copyright © Jean Jullien
& Gwendal Le Bec 2014

Published with the permission of Comme des géants inc.,
6504, av. Christophe-Colomb, Montreal (Quebec) H2S 2G8

First published in Great Britain in 2016 by Frances Lincoln
Children's Books, 74-77 White Lion Street, London N1 9PF
www.franceslincoln.com

Translation rights arranged through VeroK Agency, Spain

A catalogue record for this book is available from the British
Library.

ISBN 978-1-84780-818-9

Printed in Shenzhen, Guangdong, China

9 8 7 6 5 4 3 2 1

Ralf.

Jean Jullien

Original idea and illustrations by
Jean Jullien

Text collaboration by
Gwendal Le Bec

Frances Lincoln
Children's Books

Ralf is a little dog...

... who takes up a lot of space!

He creeps into bed and barks,

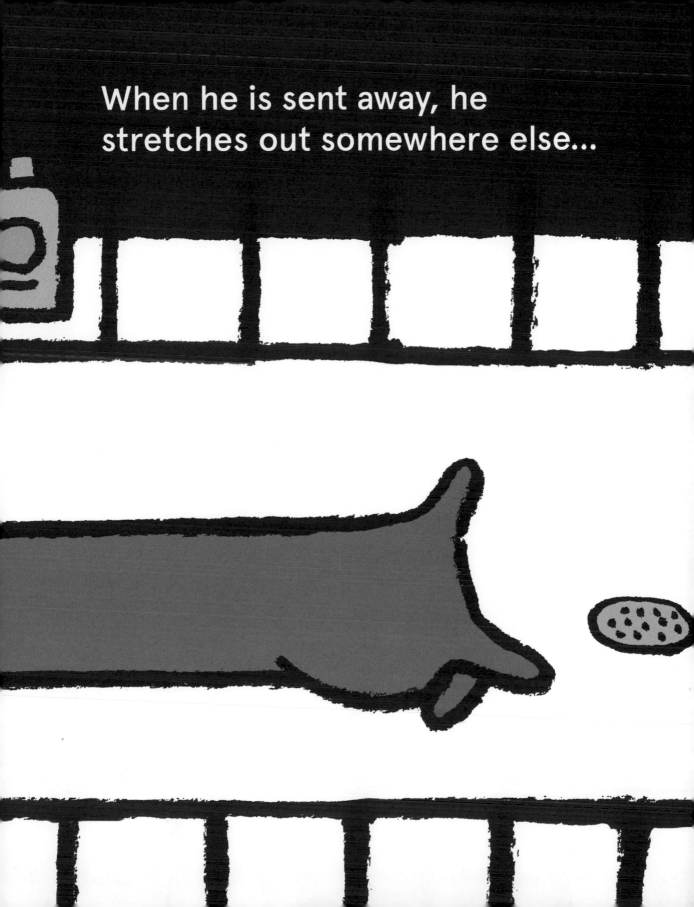

... but hardly ever in the right spot.

"Stop getting under our feet!"
we are always shouting.

But Ralf doesn't mean to cause trouble.

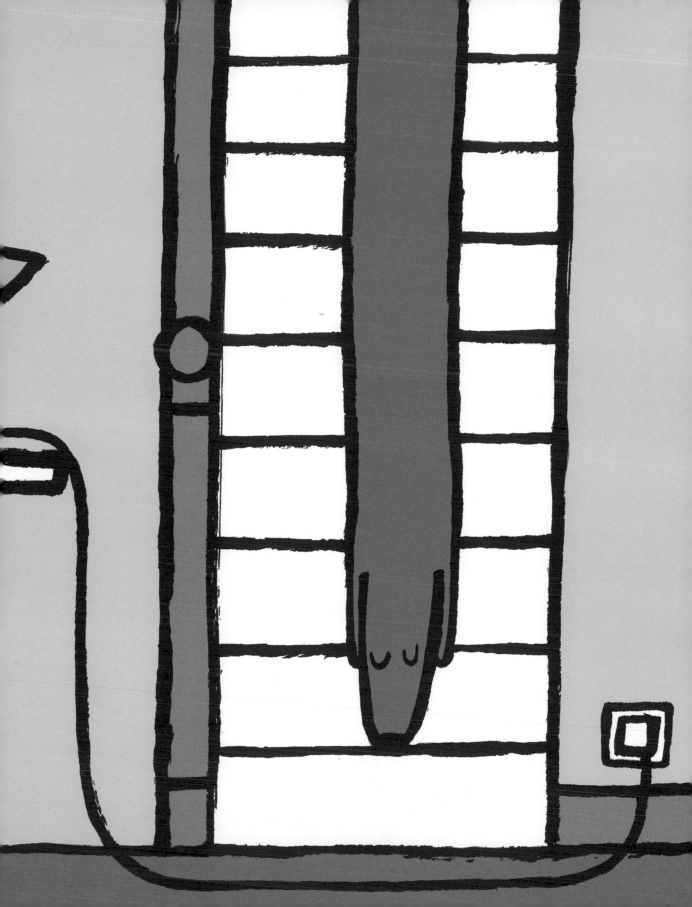

It's just that his long body gets in the way all the time.

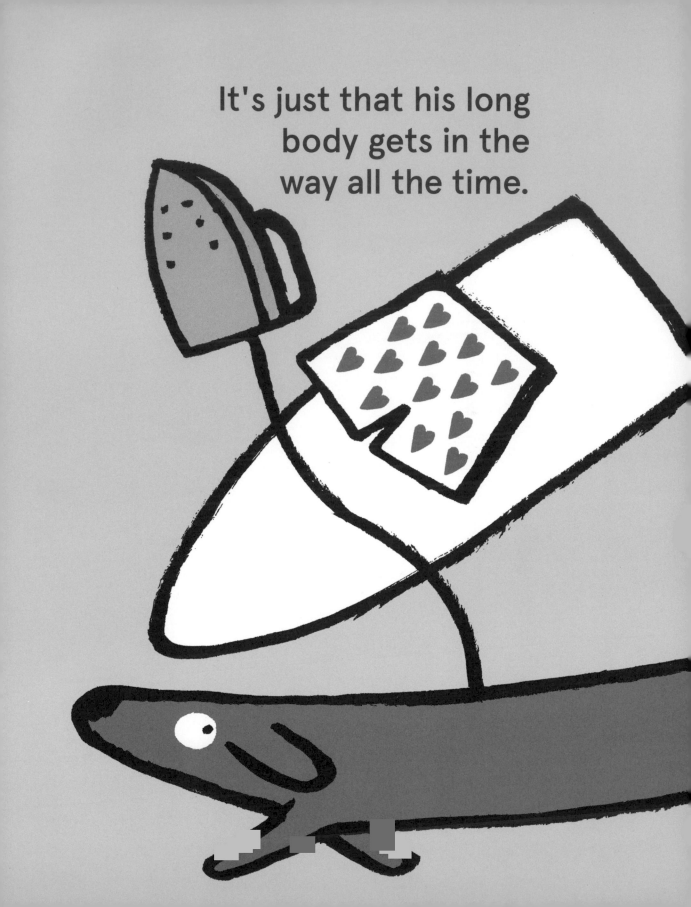

It drives Dad mad.

Maybe a bit too quiet...

Sniff! Sniff!
The smell of smoke
tickles his nose.

Quickly! Ralf runs into the house to see what's going on.

"Ouch!"
His bottom gets stuck
in the door.

But if he doesn't
do something,
the house will
burn down!

Ralf pulls so hard that his
body begins to stretch.

yone is
asleep!
t can he do?

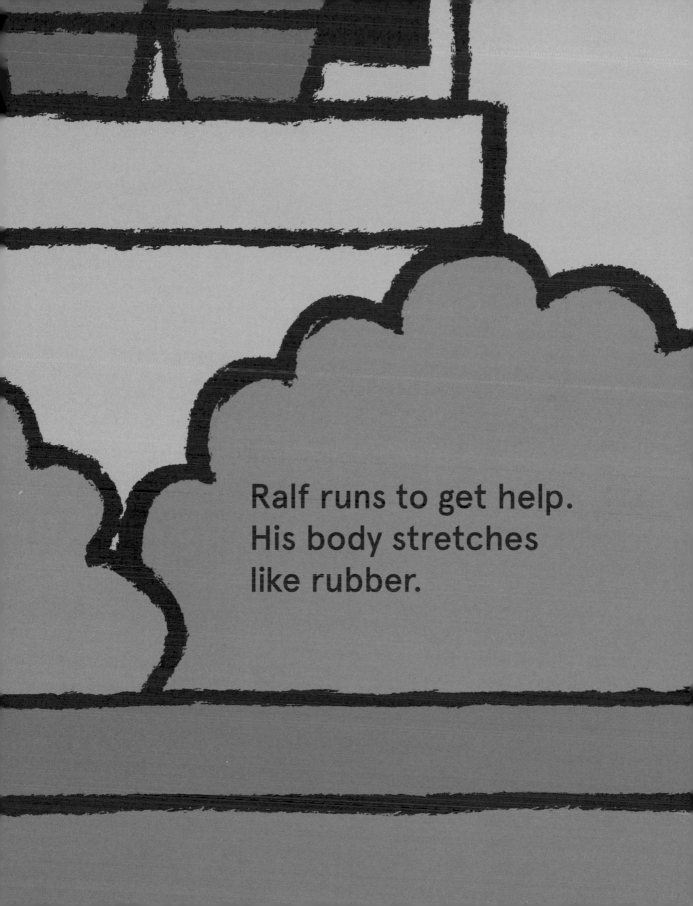

Ralf runs to get help.
His body stretches
like rubber.

WHOOSH!
Ten seconds
later, everyone
has escaped the
burning house.

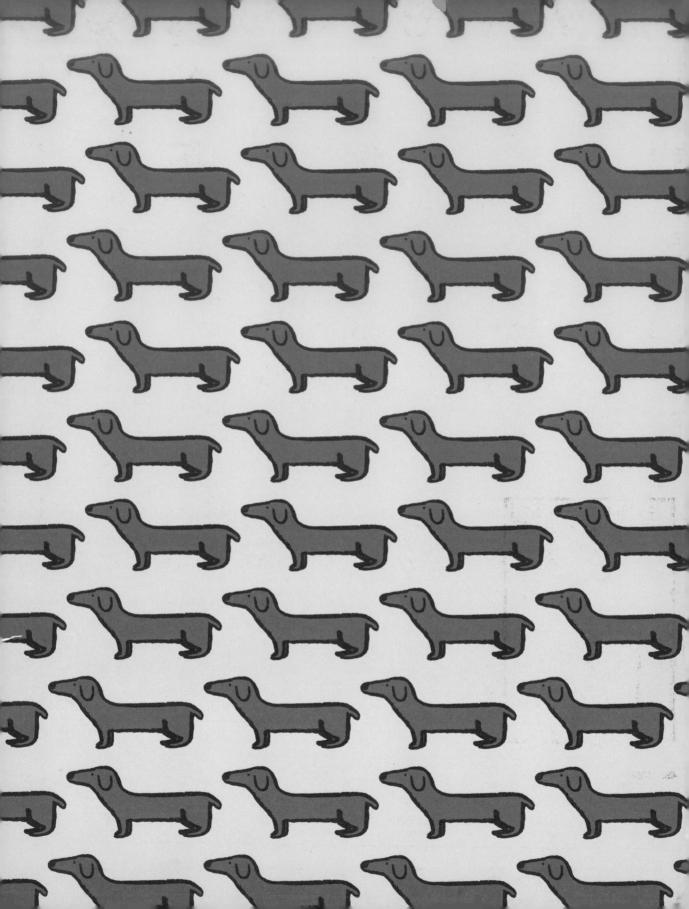